RANKA
Poems by Apostolos N. Athanassakis

[handwritten dedication in Greek]

Τοῦ Κώστα
μέ θερμούς χαιρετισμούς
ἀπό τή Σουηδία.
Ὀκτ. 1, 1978.

*Cover photograph: a painted rock by Yannis Ritsos
courtesy of Regina Pagoulatou*

RANKA

Poems

by

Apostolos N. Athanassakis

PELLA

PELLA PUBLISHING COMPANY
New York, NY 10001
1978

Other books by
Apostolos N. Athanassakis

Apeirotan (poems)

Apocolocyntosis Divi Claudii (Pumpkinification of Claudius: translation, commentary)

Vita Sancti Pachomii (translation)

The Homeric Hymns (translation and notes)

The Orphic Hymns (translation and notes)

The Judaeo-Greek Hymns of Jannina (Professor Benjamin Schwartz, co-editor)

Antilaloi tês Ziouras. Poems in Greek.

Lady of the Vineyards, by Yannis Ritsos (translation)

Library of Congress Catalog Card Number 78-060634
ISBN 0-918618-14-2

Printed in the United States of America
by
Athens Printing Company
461 Eighth Avenue
New York, NY 10001

TABLE OF CONTENTS

RAGNHILDUR

I

What do you know of blues,
whose eyes sparkle with the blue
of heaven?
What do you know of the drone
and whir of drunken bees
that crowd the mindhive
when the days are endless
and the memories of sorrow past
heave and well up against
the gray wall,
the fortress where nothingness lurks,
nothingness, whose echo is a dirge?
You, whose heart
bursts with the song of April.

II

It is what we do not say
that matters,
the mute message,
the untapped well of feeling
that caution masks with trite words.

III

O sadness that comes
for the touch that is not there,
sadness like the stillness
over a windswept plain
after the storm.
Loneliness that settles in
like a bat in some dark hollow.
The severance, the apartness,
the bond that might have been,
and then
    pains untold, cries unuttered,
    howls never raised.
All this and none of it
perhaps.

LUBBA,

boast to no one
that your charms
laid me low.
Tell no one about the mad Greek
who kept Irish wakes
over the body of love stillborn.
I am not mad
but on occasion
I happen to think
that there is a thin line
between sanity presumed
and madness declared.

AURA

Your laughter is your own,
but you share it
with gurgling streams
and babies tickled
by loving mothers.
Your beauty is your own
but you give of it,
especially to a glass
of clear water
when you hold it
as though you held
the horn of plenty.

REVERIE

I hope you're sleeping
the sleep I have not known for days.
And I hope you are dreaming
that you are a little girl picking buttercups
in some field where the grass is soft and green.
As for me:
the road is long,
and were it to take me
by your bed
I'd let you sleep on and on
and only tuck you in
if you were cold.

KALYPSO

Presumption is no small sin,
and to think that you are Odysseus
and she is Kalypso
is to overstate. Guilty of conceit —
but you've wandered from your Ithaca
and, though you've slain a few monsters,
here you are now on an island,
two years short of the magic cycle.
Foolishness knows no bounds,
and why should it?
No chance to deny the offer of immortality,
for there shall be none.
And since you are carrying
a prefabricated raft,
she may send you on your way
knowing that
you are bound for home,
where you own and are owned,
unfree to give and take
without remorse,
even when Aphrodite incarnate
demands your worship.
The hero, though, willing captive
for seven years
served as priest of love's imperative,
and here I sit,
like some wretched desert monk,
beset by ifs and buts —
That is the difference.

To reach Ithaca
without having heard the sirens
and consorted with Kalypso
is to have never left.

EYES

Eyes unseen by the vulgar,
light that makes darkness
of the brightest April day
in Greece.
Eyes demure and shy;
they light up when lips
part into a smile seen
only on *Korai*,
and a giggle, like a blend
of a mare's neighing
and an angel's song,
fills the room.
Oh do not gaze into strangers' eyes
for they rove the seas,
pirates and robbers all of them,
and you own so much —

THOR

Why does warmth of heart need
the drunk's stupor to shine through
eyes that were meant to kindle
fire?
The sore left by love forlorn
is now festering and needs the salve
of liquor to be poured over a scab
that thirsts.

Yes, they were out, the owls
of nights filled with smoke,
choking with meaningless giggles.

And as you wobbled to each one
and asked to be cuddled
and given the bottle of oblivion,
they
      they hooted in feigned disgust
      and reminded you, each in turn,
      that the last thing you need
      is pity.

HERE IN ICELAND

Here in Iceland
only the wind talks
to strangers.
And he does not whisper
a welcome in timid murmur
beneath some pine ⌣⌣
No, descending from heath
and glacier, he rushes
on his steel-hoofed pony,
mane madly tossing about,
to howl and whine
by windows not smeared with lamb blood,
to yowl like a cat in heat
strangers go home.

ICELAND

From here then I can stretch my wings
and span North and South.
From here I can scream like a Pindos eagle
and howl like the *berserkir*.
From here I can beat the primal drum
to frenzy and wake up
souls Homer would have called worthy
to form a ring of dancers
who met their death, knowing that,
even if God be not, a man need not
sink to misty darkness, like a worthless wretch.

Quick!
    Let someone bring the horn filled with mead,
or Nestor's cup brimming with wine.
        This dance, this ring
        where *drengr* and *levendis* join hands
        is not a mindless orgy
        drowned in pop and coca-cola.
        This is a feast for Europe's finest,
        kinsmen of Julian the Apostate,
        whom *Superstitio Illa*
        shamelessly called a nithing.

To him tonight let us drink
a hearty wassail,
to him,
to him who knew
who the true nithings were,
to him and Iceland,
land where the air is thick
with the ghosts of men
who laughed in the face
of Death.

MATINS

Do not seal my lips
and take song away.
Do not measure what you give me.
I have left no account unbalanced.
And if your loveliness
has made me seek your touch
and take to glossolalia,
remember: the countdown has begun,
and that when I leave
there will no longer be a madness
by which to judge your sanity.

CULPA CULPARUM—

Am I aging
or just growing up?
The spark still lingers
in my loins;
I find a woman's flesh sweet
and I yearn to leap
like a mountain goat
for that brief spasm.
Yet, when I meet a woman
who is worth the pains of hell,
I dare not touch her easily
for fear that love's dream
might dissolve
and passion misunderstood
become the dross of eros burnt
where fire was not meant to be.

NO REGRETS

I have no regrets.
As the sober morning untangles night's dreams,
I can still say you were divine,
being as you were meant to be,
"child of the earth and of the starry sky."
For this, fire of night has left no ashes
for the morning.
For this, like some priest chanting
untiringly endless benedictions,
I repeat *ou nemesis.*

ALDREI

The sun will die
before the spark of your eyes
dies in my heart.
And eternity reflected in them,
as on blue fell you gazed,
will meet its end
when, with the last heartbeat
all for me is over.

But, thief that I am,
in the hollow of my naked bones
I may carry the spark
to hell's endless night
and plunge into it
like a falling star.

LIMBO

Green was the moss of the stagnant pool
Where the water, unaware of the sun's dreams,
remained black and brooding.

There one night the red moon plunged its despair,
hoping that the aged elves would fuss with it,
or that some sprite would giggle.

But all was quiet.
The moss had forgotten to grow
and the water to move.
The path leading to it
had not been trodden upon for years.

A farmer's child that liked to throw
stones into it
now lay dead somewhere.

There was peace now.
The dreams the sun dreamt
were unwelcome nightmares,
and the pool such a grave of sarcasm
as to laugh at the red moon
that was foolish enough
to plummet to the murky depths
of such a still hellhole.

NO WORD

If only I could drown you
in a glass of red wine
and drink you to the lees.

Blessed are those whose memory
recalls only their last meal
and whose hopes go no further
than the next one.

But you, proud filly of the Icelandic prairie,
toss your mane
and lash me with the whip of memories.
To my phantom-hungry mind
this night you are a fury.

My pride is no shallow rivulet,
and I would hope
that you could remember enough
to spare me the generous measure of pity
women are wont to ration "interesting" lovers.

If only I could laugh
at the thought of merciful recollection,
Oh, if I could sing a song
to the wind
and ask it not to rap on your window,
I would sleep better,
and dreamwings would stroke
your face as gently
as my fingers once did.

PRETENSION

As doubt creeps in
pride plates the soul
            with tin,
as though it were some old copper vessel
forgotten and unused for years.

I weave my cocoon
of pretended indifference
and walk into the comfort
of its transparency,
more naked than before.

CALCULATION

Eyelids heavy
　　　with unspent sleep
shade desire
　　　in eyes liquid
with lust dammed
　　　by feline calculation.

She lies still as a spider,
watching the victim's every move,
and she is anxious to receive
　　and to give
only what feigned modesty allows.
　She measures the dole carefully
and yields in surrender to the vanquished.

EXPECTATION

I have written a hymnal to her
who once claimed to have given
herself to me.

Yet the hollow of my hands
was not empty;

the apple I held was red,
untouched by the worm of calculation,
fruit of a summer spent in search
of that distant past when an apple
would suffice.

Now summer is gone
and even fall has vanished.
Winter they call the season,
whose winds have frozen
the votive hands and the gift they clasp
into a piece of icy sculpture
that motionless awaits
the thaw of spring.

Not that spring was promised.
Silence is the way of the north.
It's just that flesh knows
as much as tree trunks.

THE GRAMMARIAN

I wove your name
into patterns of grammar and syntax,
especially conditional clauses.
Ah, what if . . .

Then I'd take
some casually scribbled note
from you,
and I'd read the weather report,
as though I were deciphering
the script of a chinese scrawl
that would finally tell me
how life and love twine,
how death can be shamed
and how a glass filled with despair
could look half empty.

WAITING

Like some sixteen-year old
waiting for his love,
the love that never comes,
I waited for you
in fretful breathlessness.
You came fairer and more crystalline
than the coolest spring,
and in my thirst for you
I asked you whether you needed
a drink.

THAT LOCK OF HAIR

Suitors will beleaguer you,
suitors who never drew blood
for you.

All of them faithless rogues
posing as priests in a temple
they'll never venerate;
all of them chanting hymns
laughed at by monkeys,
all of them lighting candles
that turn day to night.

When my bowstring breaks
don't refuse me the lock
of your russet hair,
the hair I only love.

CAUTION

You have not danced your dance,
and your seven veils, Ranka,
cling to your skin
like the seven deadly sins.

And you've asked the servants
to pickle the prophet's head
so that you may look at it later,
at your convenience.

SIMPLE THINGS ARE BEST

Today I walked on that familiar path
we'd taken the summer I met you
when I thought I could laugh
without forethought.

Simple things are best.

Today the buttercups
and every blade of grass
knew I was alone.
Last summer's laughter
hung on every gray wall
like a coat soaked in all
of last winter's rain.

Simple things are best.
But we meet and part,
thinking that grass does not wither
and that our shoes will last
forever.

THE SERPENT AND THE SHRINK

In a treeless land Aaron
climbed the Tree of Life
and like Othin
dangled from its topmost branch
for nine days and nine nights,
himself a victim to himself.

Then came a dove
with a blank piece of paper
from Sarah, who was too wound up
to write.
The dove, itself a bit confused,
quacked:
    "The worms are eating the roots;
    Quick, some pesticide!
    The dragon that drove you
    up the Yggdrasil
    is now on some shrink's couch,
    disgorging potato chips, coke bottles
    and a lot of cacodylic gaff
    about Freud, his Jewish mother
    and some waitress who told him
    that he was full of pimples."
This said, the dove
vaticinated about
trouble-laden souls and prune juice.
When Aaron woke up
the tree was gone,
the worms had turned to spaghettini
on his kitchen table.

But the dragon was still on the couch,
and Dr. Cohen assured him
that
his mother could be exorcised
with three cloves of garlic,
Freud had long been a latrine attendant,
his soul,
        such as it was,
could be overhauled
for 65 bucks an hour.
But he had to learn
to live with his pimples —

THE TRAPPIST NUN

I see you in the distance
where you have retreated
to become a Trappist nun,
because you fear speech
and think that your soul
will be broken
by the stranger's soft words.
Yet I pick up the phone
and scuff the floor,
as I watch the quicksand
on which your taunting smile
invites me to dance,
ever moving to music
played by unseen fiddlers
for clowns in the service
of a queen carved on marble
by the twilight elves.

THE POET

On what has been lived and loved
the poet feeds like a saprophyte.
He resurrects moth-eaten memories
and airs them
as a widow airs her dead husband's clothes
before she gives them to the Salvation Army.

He freezes the moment,
hoping that some new discovery
will breathe life into rows of corpses
in his vatic vault.

What I now bury
is my love,
and I write the simplest epitaph:
Here lies Chimera;
passerby, do not laugh,
her incongruity
was her loveliness.

FYLGJAN

Unwavering in your hesitance,
you are my other self.

On Greek hills
I whispered your name
like a sacred mantra,
fearing
that if I left a syllable out
a part of my soul
would become a scarecrow
in the cornfields.

Sometimes you were
a waning moon,
or a sleepless owl;
but I mostly saw you
as a wisp of light
that sundered my dreams
and hung in midair
like a strange rune.

THE FEY QUEEN

Your hair,
    in its silken softness,
    when you toss it
    over half your face
    to mask the cat in you,
    becomes the cat-o-nine-tails.

Your eyes,
    forever fixed on some thing,
    rivet me, spread-eagled,
    naked and shorn of my hair
    on the wraithed cliff of doubt.

And your face
    sometimes
    is as vague and icy
    as the glacier
    of which you are
    the fey queen
    for those endless minutes
    of supercilious whim.

THE SCULPTURE

With words
I have tried to paint you.
If I knew how to work the chisel
I'd carve your beauty
only on the whitest marble.

I do not know
whether you'd stand proud
like a caryatid,
or you'd be lying in a meadow,
surrounded
by ithyphallic satyrs
and woodland nymphs.
    Anyway,
your chiton would reveal
the silver of your right breast
and your thighs, too, would show
just a little;
        as little as when you draw your dress
        to a casually calculated point,
        as little as when, drop by drop,
        you know how to flood the heart
        with a stinging crave
        for all of you.

TELL ME FRIEND

Those who need it least
must learn patience.
Friend — tell —
are you
or are you not?
That yesterday
may-have-never-been —
could be discussed;
that tomorrow
may-never-come —
is certain.
Tell me Friend
can you arrest this day
and then ask me
to wait?

ON TOUCH

The skin knows best.
The skin knows love
better than your heart,
and your heart
better than your mind.
Minded creatures
will try to lord it over
the heart,
and skin
Every Body.
    You,
      too,
      love.

RAPE

Legs and arms
and a squeaky tummy
that never cried
"I love you"
a head crowned with bleached hair
and two blue eyes
sealed by the sign
"open at your risk"
manufactured in Hong Kong
for patients
suffering from amatory hyperesthesia
and opthalmophobia
this doll was thrown
into a trash can
by a drunkard
who tried to mess with her
and then realized
that he might get her pregnant.

CAPTIVE WORDS

Every straw has its worth,
its texture and its sound,
and every straw knows its birth,
no matter where it's found.

It takes skill to bind
the scattered straws you find
into a sheaf.

Feel your words;
listen to them
and ask them whence they come
before you arrest them
for eternity,
and they'll always be
    freedom-bound.

LONELINESS

Companion of Loneliness,
a better friend
you'll never find.

She clings to you
when all others go
and discreetly leaves
when they come.

A lady destined
to remain a faithful mistress
of those who cannot afford
to keep her.

GOD,

if you think I have sunk low,
think, too, of how hard
you must have pushed.

THE LAST SHOW

True Grief cannot be turned to tears,
and they who keen over the laughter
of those they do not mean to amuse
are not even good buffoons.

When the sole spectator of the show
admires her own reflection in the clown's teardrops
and is too rapt to toss a coin into his tawdry hat,
when she cannot hear how he grates his heart
because she's humming to her busy nail file
the time has come to bow out with grace
and circumspection,
to close the eyes to yawning ennui,
and to shut the ears before they're split
by the loud encores of claquers hired
by her to do their bit for the two bits
she never paid at the door for fear
that her total worth would be ill invested.

Misspent grief earns no gratitude,
and those who embrace and kiss statues
should know that tears that fall on their
                              [impassive faces
leave them as smooth and cold as only marble
                              [can be ⏤

TO THAT PERFECT UNION

Beauty such as yours transcends,
grace so perfect truly emends
even Grecian form —

But if beauty of body matched beauty of soul
then, Ranka, the bell would surely toll
for all of creation.

It is a goal worth the labor,
for if achieved you'll be the neighbor
to essence divine.

To that perfect union I drink a toast,
as only then I can boast
to have been your lover.

If then I hold my peace,
I should be disowned by all of Greece,
and the stones should cry out.

THE ULTIMATE

Only spent and breathless lovers,
only they and the dead
have glazed eyes.

A SUNNY DAY IN REYKJAVIK

Undulating like a woman,
whose nipple has been stroked by innocence,
the moaning sea dies on the lips of the shore,
like the whisper of a lover
who reached passion's impasse.

Baldur's brows are decked with buttercups
as he strolls about meadows
preening their verdure in the glittering sun.

Only the fish that hang on wooden scaffolds
to dry do not hear or see
how all of Iceland couples with Helios.
But as sun and air rob them
of their last drop of fluid
their desiccated bodies somehow know
that to have been alive and mute
on such a day
would have been a crueler fate.

ON RIGHT AND LEFT

Even cherubs' wings
can raise dust
if paradise is left too long
unaired and innocent —
of God's feather-duster.
And if the fallen angels
shoot cherubs down to hell,
they can make quills from their wings
to write God
how it was his right hand
    and spiraling pride
that sent them in exile
    to abysmal darkness
for their leftist views.

JUST AN X

Even passion has a peak
from which the wise descend
when to climb beyond
would mean to tread on air
and plunge down where death waits.

Since I cannot want you more
I must have less and less of you
until in your book of case histories
I am listed
as a former addict,
        an ex-convict,
        a potential ex-lover,
        or actually just as an
        X.

LOVE IMPRISONED

Wise may be those who seal their lips,
that love stay prisoner
and not be free
to spell its name.

But happy are those who never make
of their hearts sunless dungeons
and whose lips part to let love through,

transfigured as
    song
    or sigh —

RECONCILIATION

Now that I can see
all of you
I — myself — am no longer
halved.

Now I can choose to hack,
but my cleaver is gentle
and since — you — feel —
pain is not your business,
I can either cut the bond
and run to freedom,
or halve you —
and take the part
that can be had —
in honesty.
To that I pledge a love
as simple
as a baby's kiss,
as whole as all
I thought you were.

Free now of you,
my summer love,
I can from now on — and on —
be yours all winters.

BAD DEFINITION

Good to see you ⌣
inarticulate ⌣
and say nothing
to make you feel
the Woman.

Blinded by passion
I coupled ⌣ your name ⌣
with a prepositive
that lifted you
to queendom.

Trailing your language
I became postpositive:
woman-the,
I behold you mute.
Passion ⌣ my muse ⌣
gave me speech;
It attached the article
to one of a species
to rob you for a year
of your generic amplitude.
A bad definition ⌣ granted ⌣
from the start.

WATER IS BEST

Sweetened vinegar
does not cease to be
what it is,
and mead
    drunk to excess
    in nights that seem endless
    will be seen
    by morning light
    as vomit.

CONSOLATION

The vacuum
   left by emptiness
   cannot be filled,
and love that never was
cannot be turned to hatred.

      Even the rich cannot be robbed.
      Time possesses all
      and he alone inherits.

PORTRAIT

These are no thief's eyes:
Aegean blue
arrested in quartz
demands light
in which to glitter.

Cursed be every dark mood of mine
that gave their limpid blue
a somber tincture.

Lips meant to kiss babies
and lovers as innocent;
lips that quiver best
when they are motionless.

Eyes and lips
on which a lambent smile
glows, determined not to be eclipsed
by the halo of golden hair,
that circumscription of light by light.

These are no thief's eyes,
but they steal and rob
and they accept no ransom. (To Anne)

THE PINK MODEL

He felt
    blood would give
    her pale beauty
    its true color.

But
    there was so much
    of her to paint
    that the crimson hue
    faded miles before
    he could trace the path
    to the prison where
    she kept her essence.

She owed him nothing.
After all,
    he was the painter
    of the Pink Model,
    the model that had posed
    too well for blood to be
    sufficient fee.

TIME WILL DO IT

I am too intelligent
to make you smart—now.
Time will do it.
Time through wrinkle and crease
will teach you smoothness;
softness too, through hardship.
And through bony angularity
time will tell you of rondure.

Time will pluck your hair
to show you how baldness
of head or soul
is a forest of naked trees in pain.

Time will dim your eyes
so that you can see better
the sheen on the wings of blackbirds
and jet-black night.

Time the graduate
will show you how each step
of the descending ladder
may take you to heights
from which you may stoop
with pride and grace.

Yes, Ranka,
Time will teach you compassion.

CHIAROSCURO

"April is the cruelest month"
and the brightest days
are a harsher foil
for darkness that lurks within;
but evenings, too, bring little joy
to those taught by grief
that night gives the restless no respite.

Then only touch
can smooth the bristles
of the porcupine of loneliness
that marches at full tilt
to sting the quick of souls
severed from all that matters.

This is why
I want
    to stroke you so gently
    that your skin smarts with pain
    and every pore of your body
    craves to be lashed to numbness.
    The softness of my touch will tell
    how the scent your skin wafts
    is a flaming gale that consumes me
    like an insubstantial leaf.
    Yes, lie next to me
    and stay a night
    so long that morning
    never comes.

GLOSSARY

aldrei — Icel. 'never'

Baldur — Norse god. 'Baldur's brow' (Baldursbrá) is the name of the white flower *cotula foetida*, and also the brow of Baldur.

berserkir — berserks (Norse warriors who in battle were seized with frenzy; they were believed to be invulnerable).

drengr — a word which in Old Norse, especially when qualified by the epithet 'good', meant a gallant and bold man.

fylgja — in Old Norse times a 'fetch', a female guardian spirit, whose appearance foreboded one's death. In modern lore also a 'fetch' which usually appears in the shape of an animal, a crescent, or the like going before a man.

korai — the well-known 'maidens' of archaic Greek sculpture.

levendis — in Modern Greek a man who is the embodiment of such positive virtues as courage, physical beauty, generosity, defiance of death, etc.

nithing — wretch, villain.

ou nemesis — 'no blame' (Iliad 3.156), from the lines:
No blame on Trojans and
                    [fair-greaved Achaeans
if they suffer for long for the sake
                    [of such a woman.
The woman in question is the beautiful Helen.

superstitio illa   'that superstition', a contemptuous phrase used of christianity by the Roman historian Tacitus.

Yggdrasil   in Norse mythology the ash tree symbolizing the universe.